W9-CEW-132

READ IT AND PASS IT ON!
BERNIESBOOKBANK.ORG

For Richard, Frances, Rachel, Joseph, Theo, Araba, Tom, Jenny, Ana, and Jack
G.L.

For all my family in Germany
(Für meine ganze Familie in Deutschland)
K.L.

Library of Congress Cataloging-in-Publication Data

Lobel, Gillian.
Moonshadow's journey / Gillian Lobel ; illustrated by Karin Littlewood.
p. cm.
Summary: When his beloved grandfather is killed in a storm while leading the swan flock south for the winter,
Moonshadow is reassured by his father that the flock will go on with Grandfather always in their hearts.
ISBN 978-0-8075-5273-5
[1. Swans—Fiction. 2. Birds—Migration—Fiction. 3. Grandfathers—Fiction. 4. Death—Fiction.] I. Littlewood, Karin, ill. II. Title.
PZ7.L7798Mo 2009 [E]—dc22 2009000004

Text copyright © 2009 by Gillian Lobel. Illustrations copyright © 2009 by Karin Littlewood.
Published in 2009 by Albert Whitman & Company, 6340 Oakton Street, Morton Grove, Illinois 60053-2723.
All rights reserved. No part of this book may be reproduced or transmitted in any form or by any means, electronic or mechanical,
including photocopying, recording, or by any information storage and retrieval system, without permission in writing from the publisher.
Printed in Indonesia.
10 9 8 7 6 5 4 3 2 1

First published in Great Britain in 2009 by Gullane Children's Books.

For more information about Albert Whitman & Company,
visit our web site at www.albertwhitman.com.

# Moonshadow's Journey

Written by
## Gillian Lobel

Illustrated by
## Karin Littlewood

Albert Whitman & Company, Morton Grove, Illinois

High above the earth flew the swans. White wings
feathered the wind, and the air was loud with their joyful cries.
"Going South!" they said. "To the warm sun and the green fields."
Moonshadow shivered with excitement as he watched,
snuggled up close to his grandfather.

"When are we going, Grandfather?" he asked.
"Very soon, Moonshadow!" said Grandfather.
"But where are we all going?"
"To the warm lands, Little One; it is
much too cold for us here in the winter."
"Will I—will I be able to fly that far?" Moonshadow wondered.

"Yes, my Little One. I will lead you,
by sun and stars, as my father did before me."
Gently Grandfather nibbled at Moonshadow's feathers.
And Moonshadow knew that everything would be all right.

Suddenly, from the North, a fierce, cold wind blew.
The flock stirred, beating their wings and straining their necks.
"Now!" cried Grandfather. "The time is right!" And he began the
strong, slow run to take off, his wings beating the air.
Moonshadow ran like the wind . . .

And then he was up, up, and away, high in
the blue, leaving the icy marshes below him.

He flew close to his mother and father, lifted on the strong upbeat of the circling wings. All through the night they flew, pale shadows in the moonlight, over the cold brown lands, through the stinging snowflakes, on, on, never stopping.

Sunrise washed their feathers with gold and rose, and still
they flew, over the sleeping towns, over rooftops and domes,
until the land slipped away, and they came to the wrinkled sea.

The little swan beat his wings fiercely, trying so
hard not to slip behind. A burning ache filled his body.

Grandfather knew that his little
ones were weary. Whooping loudly, he
spiraled downwards to a tiny island.

Moonshadow sighed with relief. How good it was
to slide along the water and furl his wings! He
gazed up at the stars blazing overhead. And then
he saw a wonder . . .

The sky was lit by sheets of swirling lights.
"What is it, Father?" cried Moonshadow.
"The Dancing Lights of the North," said Father. "They shine for us!"
"Now sleep," said Mother. "You have a long journey ahead."
Moonshadow watched until his eyelids drooped, and he fell
into a deep sleep. But Grandfather stayed awake, guarding his flock.

At sunrise, they were off again. Moonshadow felt new strength flow into his wings. That day, the flying was easy. But when night came, the air froze, and the stars disappeared. How would Grandfather guide them now?

The wind grew fierce, and lightning ripped the clouds. For a second the whole flock glowed white. Then the sky roared, and hard balls of ice beat against Moonshadow's head. He could no longer hear the beat of his parents' wings.

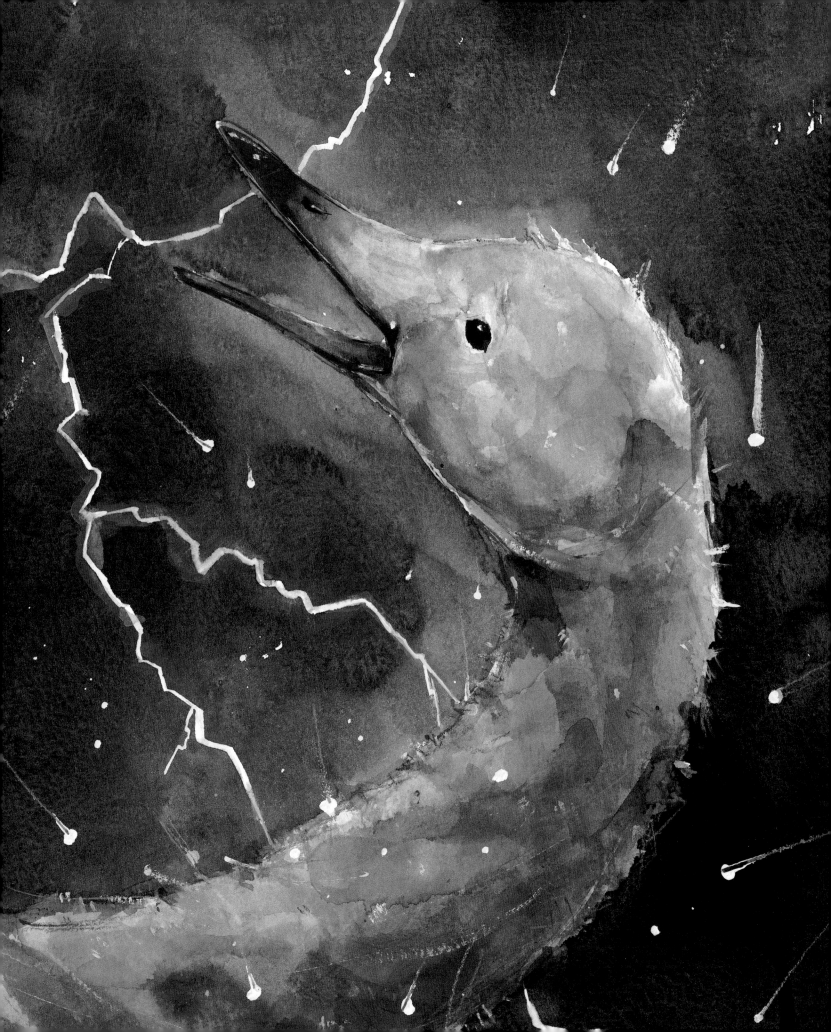

"Mother! Father!"
he cried in terror.
"Where are you?"
He started to fall,
spinning down, down.

And then he felt strong wings beneath
him and knew that his mother and father
were there, drawing him on with the power
of their wings and the strength of their love.

Slowly the wind dropped, and the air softened. They saw
land and flew down to rest. Moonshadow looked all around.
"Mother!" he gasped. "I can't see Grandfather!"

"He fell in the storm," said his mother sadly.

Moonshadow's heart overflowed with sorrow.
"Who will lead us now, Father?" he cried.
"I will," said his father. "Follow me, my son.
We must go on, even though our hearts are heavy."

Over the purple moors they flew, over green hills and
checkered fields. And just as the sun was setting and
Moonshadow felt he could go on no longer, they
came to a place of great shining waters.

Moonshadow's father began a slow, wide circle, then started the final slide to the silver lake. Suddenly Moonshadow was down, too. The whole flock whooped with joy. Moonshadow dipped his beak into the water and sipped the rich, good food.

Great trees fringed the lake, glowing amber and gold.
Moonshadow fluffed out his feathers. All around him,
his family glided over the lake. No—not all his family:

Grandfather was not there.
Moonshadow's heart ached, and he hung his head.

His father caressed him gently.
"Grandfather will always be in our hearts, where
nothing can take him from us, Moonshadow. And the flock
will go on. I will lead now—as one day you will, my son."

Moonshadow looked proudly at his father.
Then, safe and warm in the heart of his family,
he tucked his head under his wing, and slept.

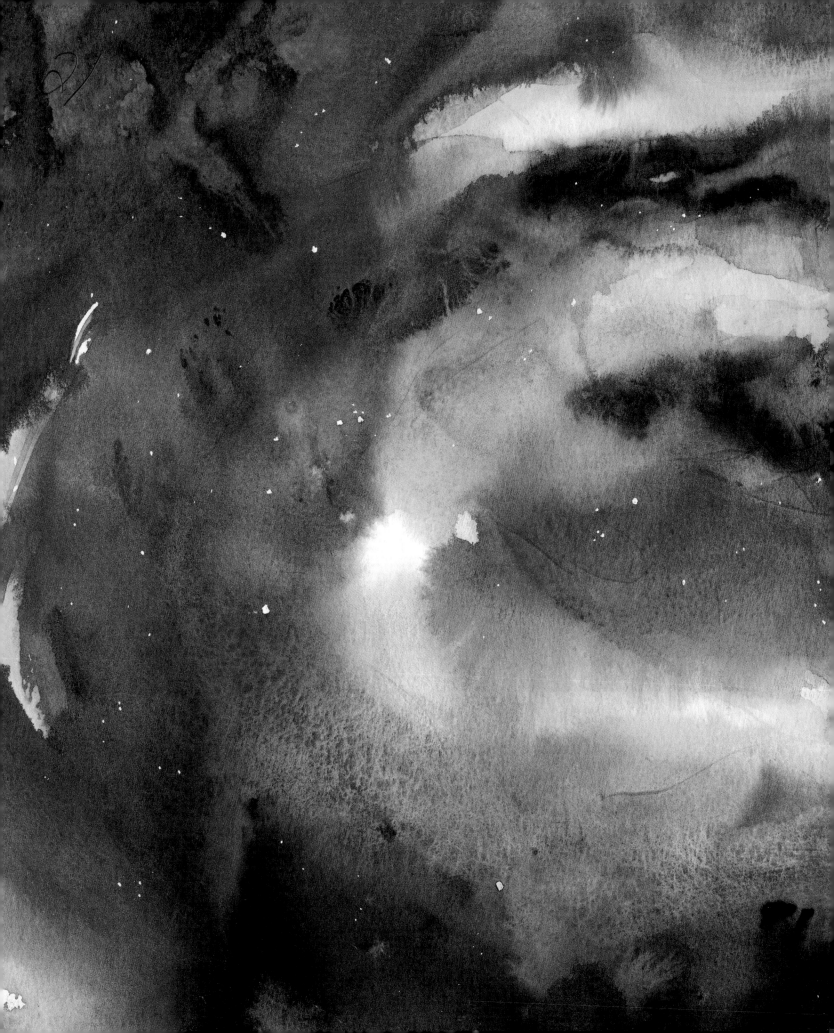